The Things
We Fear Most

The Things We Fear Most

stories

GLORIA VANDERBILT

Library and Archives Canada Cataloguing in Publication

Vanderbilt, Gloria [date]
    The things we fear most : stories / Gloria Vanderbilt.

ISBN 978-1-55096-129-4

    I. Title.

PS3572.A42828T55 2011   813'.54   C2011-902937-5

Design and Composition by Michael Callaghan
Cover photograph by Allison Saathoff
Typeset in Garamond and Lucida fonts at the Moons of Jupiter Studios
Printed by Friesens

Printed and Bound in Canada in 2011
Published by Exile Editions Ltd.
144483 Southgate Road 14 – GD
Holstein, Ontario, N0G 2A0

Canadian Sales Distribution: U.S. Sales Distribution:
McArthur & Company   Independent Publishers Group
c/o Harper Collins   814 North Franklin Street
1995 Markham Road   Chicago, IL 60610
Toronto, ON M1B 5M8   www.ipgbook.com
toll free: 1 800 387 0117   toll free: 1 800 888 4741

In loving memory of S.L.

CONTENTS

The Things
We Fear Most

THE HOUR BETWEEN

I was gathering tulips in the garden, finding happiness in beauty as my love lay in the grass beside me. Muffled at first, then unmistakably intruding into our lazy conversation – sounds of bees – no, something else. A voice that sounded like mine, but it was his, far and away, coming from a face distorted as by a mirror in a fun house. But it is not him, it's mine too, struggling to prevent a quarrel that fast accelerates into a roller coaster speeding over the top, on down, crashing, unable to stop.

It took four men to place it in the bay window of our dining room – an aviary. We marveled at the delicacy of line conceived by a master builder, a castle of lacy wire arabesques painted white for lovebirds to inhabit. But touching, there was chill, a bitter taste of steel. Later my love found paroquets from Uruguay, yellow as butter and black of eye. Close, close, home he brought the pair, yellow, so black of eye, he set them free to inhabit the aviary, standing, his arm around me, kissing me as the paroquets nestled on the perch.

I knew about it from the beginning, and sometimes wondered if anyone else did? The hours between light and dark – to be feared, because the day has ended and what night may bring has not yet happened.

The bell tower chimes five as I stand in the snow turning the key into the lock. Streetlight filters into the dark house, spirals of snow hiss on panes of glass melting into nothingness. Far down the corridor the white aviary stands outlined against the bay window. Snow appears to be swirling into the house, bursting into sun-drenched crystals, and everywhere the sounds of birds making love. I hasten towards our garden of Eden, but sudden – silence. Then laughter. Has he gone to another rendezvous (that may or may not happen)? Holding my breath I wait for the hour between to end, but I can't. Pressing

forward I peer into the aviary – no birds yellow
there, no birds black of eye but two strange creatures,
necks entwined, beaks embedded in each other they
lie on the floor of the cage, yellow feathers drenched
with blood, tucked neatly in a bed of snow.

THE EYELET LACE DRESS

Phoebe went to Los Angeles for a two-week visit with her estranged mother the summer she was seventeen, packing in her suitcase a white eyelet party dress. She had coveted the dress in the window of Best & Co., never imagining to own it. But she did – soon after – a birthday present from her stingy, rich Aunt Emmy with whom she had been sent to live soon after her father died and her mother tooted off on a wild goose chase. But now her mother, having married and divorced a Texas tycoon, had settled down in Los Angeles where, in a Bel Air mansion, she was reinventing herself into a Beverly Hills socialite. The dress had spaghetti straps with eyelet lace flouncing in tiers, making a full skirt that swirled when she gazed in wonder at herself, pirouetting in the mirror. She had worn it only once before leaving, when her boyfriend Pete took her dancing for the first time at the Starlight Roof at the Waldorf Astoria where

Xavier Cougat's big band orchestra was playing. Pete was a senior at Princeton and he was crazy about that dress. "Oh honey," he'd said and, speechless, had circled her in his arms as they moved around the dance floor to the Cuban rhythms.

Later they went back to Aunt Emmy's house on Fifth Avenue and sneaked up to the top floor where the rooms were dark, unused, the furniture covered in sheets. They had been there many times before – a hideaway, unbeknownst to Aunt Emmy. Although Phoebe wanted more Pete was adamant that they wait, holding it as a cherished trust, sacred for their wedding night. The promise of this thrilled her, and each time he touched her and they both cried out in joy, she knew Pete was right, they should wait, because when it did happen surely it would be miraculous, for then they would truly belong to each other.

Since living with Aunt Emmy her mother had only made sporadic trips to visit Phoebe in New York, keeping in touch with postcards from faraway places, and so when Phoebe arrived in Los Angeles, her excitement turned to apprehension when her mother did not meet her at the airport, sending instead a chauffeur to pick her up. Phoebe sat back in the air-conditioned beige Mercedes looking through the windows as they drove through relentless sunlight along streets lined with palm trees, past houses with neat gardens until the car stopped at gates leading into the secluded enclave called Bel Air. A guard let them through and the chauffeur made his way up to a house that looked like an antebellum mansion in a movie. "Welcome home, Miss Phoebe," the chauffeur said, giving her suitcase to the butler, who handed it to the maid, who said, "Mrs. Frayne is asleep, but she's expecting you Miss Phoebe – please follow me," and they went up the curving staircase to a landing, on down a corridor into a room where her suitcase was placed on a folding rack at the foot of a bed canopied in dotted swiss. The maid started to unpack her suitcase, but Phoebe said, "Oh, no thanks, I'll do it myself." "As you wish," the maid replied, opening the armoire to indicate hangers padded with flowered chintz before leaving. Phoebe opened her suitcase, shook out the ruffles on the eyelet dress, and hung it in the closet, leaving the rest of her things to unpack later. She sat on the bed gazing around the room – silvered tables on either side of the bed holding crystal bowls of fluffy flowers, a white carpet needlepointed with pink cabbage roses, a chaise upholstered in pink and white stripes, the walls covered in crisp white linen. She kept thinking of Aunt Emmy's house, dark, filled with antiques as if a museum. She had never seen a room so fresh, so white, so perfect, so filled with sunlight. Phoebe dared speculate her mother had decorated it especially for her. She went to the open window and looked down into the garden – nothing moved except sprinklers on the lawn, round and round they went, mesmerizing her by sprays of water catching rainbows from the sun, as they spattered the lawn with dew. Hours later – but it was only a few minutes – there was a knock on the door and the maid was back saying, "Mrs. Frayne will see you now," and she followed her down another long corridor into her mother's room.

Her mother sat under flowered Porthault sheets, a white wicker breakfast tray over her lap, shining dark hair fanned around her shoulders. Phoebe had never seen her mother without makeup until now. It was difficult to connect her to the person she had seen the last time they met. She appeared luminous, her skin translucent, features blunted as though partly erased.

"Catkin, there you are." Her mother held out her arms, calling out, "No – no wait a minute – stand back, let me take a look at you." Phoebe stood still, but after a quick glance her mother said, "Well – we'll have to do something with your hair. Tulio is coming later to do mine for the party I'm giving tonight – he's genius, pure genius – and he'll do something with yours – the party is for you, Catkin – and *tout* Hollywood is turning out. Now – let's see what you've brought to wear," and ringing for the maid to take the tray, she jumped out of bed, threw a marabou robe over charmeuse nightgown, slid coral-lacquered toes into pom-pommed mules and, giving Phoebe a hug, took her hand and led her on back down the corridor into the guest room from which Phoebe had come.

"What's this?" her mother said, going to the closet, taking the eyelet lace dress, holding it up, shaking her head. "Phoebe – where in God's name did *this* come from?"

"It's really pretty, Mummy – once you see it on."

"But you're not a baby anymore, Catkin," her mother said, casting it onto the bed.

"It's the only party dress I came with—"

"Well – it won't do – come, let's see what we can come up with." Phoebe followed her mother into another room, which was her dressing room. Closets lined the walls, and a mirrored vanity table was cluttered with tortoiseshell boxes, a silver hand mirror engraved with her mother's initials, crystal bottles with enameled stoppers and other accoutrements Phoebe could not identify. She longed to examine in detail everything on the table, but her mother was flinging open doors of the closets to reveal an array of dresses, shoes, and accessories arranged according to color in perfect order. Her mother examined the racks of clothes, contemplating the possibilities – taking out one dress after another while Phoebe breathlessly waited.

"How about this?" she finally said, holding up a dress of lavender silk printed with – hothouse orchids? Phoebe wasn't sure. The dress had a bare midriff and her mother was shaking it enticingly at Phoebe.

"Oh Mummy, that's so beautiful!"

"Bet it fits perfectly – try it on."

Phoebe hurried out of her traveling clothes and stood naked in front of the full-length mirrors while her mother slipped the dress over her head.

"How about that!" Her mother stood back as Phoebe stood enthralled.

"Is that me?" She kept laughing, hugging herself. "But I don't think I brought the right shoes?"

"Shoes? Shoes? We'll get to that later – it's the hair we have to deal with – Tulio will really have to do something about that—"

And so he had. Hours later Phoebe found all problems solved by Tulio who spiced up her hair with a rinse, styled over a "rat," swept into a lush roll and sprayed with scented lacquer. It looked just like the hair of a film star she had seen in a movie magazine. She was thrilled by the way it framed her face, pancaked and powdered by Tulio before green shadow had been administered – "to pop those hazel eyes," he enthused. Carried away by his creation, he had crested her eyebrows with black pencil, painstakingly gluing on false eyelashes. "Voila!" He exclaimed, pulling her to stand in front of him as they gazed into the mirror. "I wonder who *that* is?" he said proudly. Wondering herself, she couldn't stop smiling.

Soon after, holding a fluted glass of champagne, Phoebe, wearing the orchid dress, stood beside her mother outfitted in strapless bouffant ruby-red gauze, the shining hair bound by a mesh snood sprinkled with diamanté, skin glittering with silver, lips outlined in blazing-red lipstick, features no longer blurred, but brought into hard focus. Phoebe couldn't stop staring at her as she greeted each new arrival, saying, "This is my daughter, Phoebe," laughing as if relieved to have a presentable one. Guests were overflowing the house, spilling out into the gardens illuminated by Japanese lanterns hanging from trees, candlelit tables covered in billowing clouds of organdy, centered with wicker baskets filled with white peonies, the pool iridescent in the moonlight as candles in flower cups floated on the aquamarine water. Phoebe had never seen so many people energized by success together in one place at the same time; there were movie stars, directors, producers, the wives who looked vaguely familiar, but why? More than anything she wanted was to be part of it – to belong. Could she? Everyone was smiling, asking how long she was going to stay? Inviting her here and there. She had never in her life felt so important.

Next day the phone kept ringing, netting her into a new life. There were lunches at Romanoffs, Sunday buffets by swimming pools, days at Malibu

on the beach, playing tennis. Drives to Palm Springs,
a Spanish fiesta in Santa Barbara where she wore her
mother's black mantilla. Yachting trips to Catalina,
shopping on Rodeo Drive where Phoebe's mother
told her to pick out dresses she fancied, Saturday
night dancing at Mocambo or Ciros. All the fellows
in town after her, until her mother, joking she was
so sought after she better have her own phone, had
promptly installed one in Phoebe's bedroom. The
days slipped by. Aunt Emmy and New York faded
and Pete, her dear Pete, seemed someone she had
known long ago when they were both children.
Soon it would be time to go back, to the ever-vigilant
cold Aunt Emmy, whom she now perceived as a
wicked witch waiting to take happiness away. Here
she was allowed to go, see, do anything she wanted
– there were no boundaries. That's what it meant to
be grown-up, wasn't it? She didn't have to run deci-
sions by her mother, preoccupied as she was by a
new girlfriend. Heaven, but sometimes hell – adrift
in a dark sea not knowing how to navigate, yearning for her mother's attention. Still – as time grew
near to leave she begged not to have to go back.

"But of course, Catkin," her mother said. "Stay
as long as you like."

"But Aunt Emmy – what about her?" Phoebe said, panic-stricken.

"Well, what about Aunt Emmy?" Her mother was annoyed. "You're a big girl now; what's she going to do – have someone kidnap you and return you?"

"But who's going to tell her?" Phoebe couldn't imagine she would have to be the one to do it.

"Leave it to me," her mother said briskly.

The way her mother presented it – it sounded so simple. And it was. She just stayed on and soon became intrigued with an actor a lot older – thirty-six, maybe older? He was British and dashing and worked from time to time in B-movies. Her mother wasn't particularly interested except to comment he was a bit of a bounder, but she didn't question Phoebe's going out with him or any other of the men buzzing around her. On their first date he took her to Trader Vic's and ordered Navy Grogs. She had never tasted rum before and it gave her a feeling of confidence, so when he ordered seconds she didn't say no. After dinner he said, "Let's go to Santa Monica Pier, have a spin." When they got there, she found herself in a basket, suspended on a wheel whirling round and round, dizzy as she gripped his hand, closing her eyes and trying to block out the fact that she was kissing him instead of Pete. After that they drove to his house in the Valley and she sprawled on the bed, falling asleep, but he would have none of that as he unzipped his pants and pulled up her skirt.

"Hey, hey there, calm down. The neighbors will hear you – don't want to get me into trouble do you? San Quentin Quail – you know," he laughed, trying to jolly her out of it.

"And who the hell is Pete? No one ever cried for me like that. Here – take this," and he handed her a towel to stop the bleeding.

But Phoebe couldn't stop sobbing, and when morning came she found somehow he'd gotten her home, for there she was, naked under the canopy of the bed in her mother's house. The clothes she'd worn the night before in a pile on the floor. The phone ringing—

Later when Phoebe saw him at parties in a crowd she pretended she didn't know he was there. She soon started seeing others, but when they made love to her she didn't cry because it didn't matter any-more.

That summer the eyelet dress hung unworn in the back of the closet, but eventually Phoebe passed it along to the housekeeper who gave it to her daughter. All that had happened a long time ago, of course, but while thoughts of the actor were pushed from her mind – Pete for some reason stayed in it forever.

MY LITTLE MOUSE

My little mouse he slipped away down the road one end of day ... down, down the road I watched him sway, slow, so slow, it seemed he waited for a hand from me. Try as I would not one could move, so faint was I from where I stood. Now faraway at end of day sometimes, I look and look. Where did he go? That little mouse I shook and shook who loved me so, and does he too turn back to look?

Although no longer together we still live in the same city my little mouse and I. And thirty blocks from where I live stands the building and the rooms we lived in together long ago. Now others claim them, and, although we knew it not at the time, the buildings and rooms we now separately inhabit – waited.

Opening my refrigerator I stare at the bottle of apple juice on the top shelf, and come aware of a stone-cold fact: in buildings and rooms in other cities (even perhaps across the street), others live, unaware, as we are, that someday we may be living in that very room because rooms wait for us – rooms where terrible things/joyous things will happen as they did long ago for me and my little mouse in the room thirty blocks away, where joy and misery drew us into a net that became a mesh of steel, blood circling, spreading as it sifted through, leaving as days led one into the other, sediments of gold and nuggets of dark pain. Passing through the planet we vacate rooms, moving on to rooms that wait to become a transient home.

Puzzling over this gives pause as I stand looking at the bottle of apple juice, asking why, for over a year as if treasuring a relic of holy water I have kept it on the top shelf inside my refrigerator? And what had possessed me calling my little mouse after years of silence asking to see him for there was something I urgently needed to tell him, yet jolted when the doorbell rang to find him actually materialize as if in answer to a wish – from a genie out of a bottle?

There he sat in my living room on the sofa beside me, on his hand a band of gold (not mine) encircling his heart? The intensity as it was long ago when the energy of my little mouse arrowed into the center of my heart as it beat within its tiny iceberg, exploding into blazing sun … I'd forgotten how I'd missed that warmth since down the road I watched him sway. Forgotten too how before at end of day in that other room – not my little mouse, but a monkey on my back, at me for not giving him *all* of myself – denying, knowing it was true.

Surprised to find how capable of presenting myself calm, serene without collapsing to the floor as I tried to tell him how sorry at how I'd behaved at times so long ago, how sorry I was to put off having the children he longed for. "Intense that would have been," he touched my hair, almost kissing me sitting in this room that waited, as had that room in a building thirty blocks away long ago, when my little mouse I shook and shook, silently screaming out infidelities of intent – knowing *he* had been true – always.

"But I was never angry with you, pain, yes, but never anger," taking my hand, "because I knew you were searching."

I turned away.

He got up, pacing around the room looking at the clock. Did he recognize the gift he'd placed long ago on the mantel? I followed him on out into the hall and we stood silent waiting for the elevator, his arm around starting to kiss me, but the elevator door opened – I should have gone in, after him. Or run down the flight of back stairs to be waiting as he emerged. But I didn't think of that until after.

Next day when the phone rang I knew it was him.

"Great seeing you, you looked beautiful – would love to see you again – maybe Tuesday?"

"Yes, yes Tuesday, I'd love that."

"Is there a deli near? Could order chicken sand-wiches on rye, Russian dressing, coleslaw, apple juice."

"Yes, just around the corner—"

I put down the phone and went to look in the mirror. The face looking back at me was someone else, but who I was, hard put to say? Opening the drawer where I kept my jewelry I reached inside to the back and pulled forth our wedding rings, each inscribed with the other's name. I hastened on out to D'Ags, purchased a bottle of apple juice, laugh-ing as I ran home at the label, *Apple and Eve Organics 100% Apple Juice*, popped it into the fridge to be icy-cool for the Tuesday arrival.

Who lives in those rooms where once we dwelled with the terrace a garden of earthly delights looking out over the river? Who treads where, try as I would, I could not move. How still it was above the city at dusk, my soul suspended, fragmented by a look, for a split-second, I broke through and gave *all* of myself, but try as I could so faint was I from where I stood, I slipped back into the secret place where my little mouse couldn't find me.

Another call. "People flying in from Paris to meet on business – not sure about lunch Tuesday – will call you next week – we have to be very careful. I'm very susceptible to you."

"Don't be afraid – I'm scared too."

Then another message: "People flying out – God, I'd love to see you. Take care."

The long wait through the weekend … Monday, morning mail – a rush of light at the familiar hand-writing.

I look and look envisioning him in a room I know not of, as he sat writing the letter. Too late, too late

– that little mouse I shook and shook. "I've been wrestling all week whether to call or not to call you. The fact that I want to so badly is precisely why I've decided I mustn't." Yes, it is clear to me now, my little mouse has slipped away into another room with another mouse (but none like me). "There is no way I could alter my life so radically if I began to see you again. It would pull my whole life apart. You know how much you've meant to me. The resonance of that is still there." Where did he go my little mouse? "There is nothing you could ask of me that I wouldn't give if I had it. So please think of me fondly as I do of you. And forgive my desire for a peaceful time for the remaining years." Yes, end of day and my little mouse has already left.

Wait. Wait. I cautioned, but to no avail, compelled words rushed onto the page. "Great gift – tell you things on my mind these many years – in my heart in friendship and love always—" something like that, can't remember so frantic to make contact—

Hands on fire I sealed the letter. Down the stairs falling into the street as I ran to the mailbox to catch the next pickup at four – ink dissolving the name on the envelope. Tears? No, drops of rain. Stumbling back up to my room. *Apple and Eve* – out – out.

But opening the fridge the lone bottle of apple juice looked familiar, so at home sitting there – I changed my mind. Best let it rest there a while—

It gives trust in the rooms that wait, rooms we don't know exist but they do. Things will happen in those rooms, with people who may or may not be strangers. Terrible things, too, but great good things will happen also. Because they do ... far and away at end of day another room waits.

MURDER

The first came two weeks apart, and later not at all. Then frequently. The dream of a murder committed while asleep. Beside me in the bed, he took me in his arms as I woke screaming. Each time he was blessedly beside me. Until one day he was not. Now I'll never find him.

INTERIOR DESIGN

Sara and David's living room needed painting, but you paint one room, and then the rest of the apartment looks not quite up to it, so it's time to paint another, and so on, until floors are being scraped, furniture reupholstered. It's as if a bomb has fallen and so you move to a hotel until everything is put back together again.

Actually it was Sara who moved to the hotel. David took the opportunity to mince down to Florida to visit his mother, eager to add to his list of grievances about her. Sara felt relief when he left. She had her own list of complaints. One being his refusal to let her take the TV dinners he favored out of their plastic containers and serve them on one of her pretty china plates. But how intriguing these quirks had once been, everything about him blessed with mystery and discovery. The withdrawn silences lasting sometimes for days added to the fascination. She had thought him a modern Heathcliff.

How difficult he was to circulate with. There was her closest friends' garden wedding when he wandered off behind the shrubberies, appearing an hour later to find her in a panic as to his whereabouts, with his excuse being, "But I don't know any of these people." To appease him they had left before the reception "because of David's sensitive stomach," Sara had apologized later.

What do you see in him? Sara's friends were too supportive to voice this, but she knew what they must be thinking. If only they could know how knockout fantastic he became when the sun went down and as lovers they met in the secret dark. A frog prince? Yes – why not? And that made up for everything. Almost.

It had taken time to adjust to his inability to sleep through the night in their bed. No chance of reaching to find a warm toe or waking at dawn in each other's arms. "Never been able to fall asleep with anyone next to me," his very words. And that was that. Then the random sloppiness of clothes in piles on the floor for the housekeeper to forage through, sort out, launder and put back on shelves in the closet Sara had organized to hold his things. As for her things, they irritated him, and, one by one over the months, they had been stored in boxes and put away.

With David out of sight, both adrift temporarily, Sara – ensconced in the anonymity of a hotel, alone through the white nights – became obsessed with the redecorating. Dare she risk some changes in David's home office? The Black Hole with its morass of papers, books, mail inundating his desk, his iMac in an avalanche of debris. Tabloid pictures of those unfortunate Collier brothers buried in the aftermath of a tornado of the mess they had created around themselves kept intruding into the beauty she was planning. Unobservant, David might not even notice if the murky cement gray walls of his home office were whisked over with a light wash of soothing café au lait, soft carpeting for his cherished feet? Then on to tidy the room, clear his mind, steer him towards connecting more efficiently with the network of enterprises with which he preoccupied himself, horsing around behind the closed door. Sara see-sawed about the advisability of this, finally deciding to "leave it where Jesus flang it" as her grandmother would say.

The decision to leave it where it had already been flung freed her to concentrate on the task at

hand. By day she made the contractor's life a living
· hell supervising the work in progress. Color changes
to reevaluate, changes about crucial details such as
which doorknobs, light switches and so on. By night
she lay in the dark of the hotel energized, minutely
going over each room, arranging and rearranging
the furniture, recovering upholstery, taking remembered treasures out of the stored boxes and placing
them on the polished gleam of surfaces. The pictures in silver frames, the basket of golden fish, the
burl collection of apples and pears lined with silver
tea paper, her grandmother's dressing table set of
pink enamel brush, comb, the powder boxes finding
pride of place in the new life. No more eating TV
dinners out of plastic dishes – not in that dining
room. But what about nightly forays back and forth
to the kitchen for junk food? The Hostess Twinkies,
the M&M's, the Fritos? The discards of half-eaten
candy bars, awaiting when she went to make coffee?
Sara doubted David would give those up. Back and
forth, forth and back during the night, fitfully
anticipating him as he pads down the hall, thirsty
and hungry from pot enjoyed during lovemaking.
Why did she feel vaguely guilty that she had no
interest in experimenting with this pleasure?

The day arrived when David called and Sara could no longer put off telling him the painters were out, furniture back several weeks ago in fact.

Sara was waiting in the hall when the key turned in the lock and there he was. He looked different, was it the hat? Some sort of goofy souvenir cap he'd picked up in the airport in Orlando? Without saying anything, he walked past her on down the hall to the door of his office. He nodded, confirming all was exactly as he had left it. His face impossible to read as he went through the apartment taking in each room, its creamy calm beauty, everything in order, everything in place, with Sara following behind silently screaming – Idiot! Don't you know decorating is autobiography and you just won't *do*.

But when he turned toward her, she smiled and said, "Welcome home."

A month later David moved out and in time she met someone at a dinner party who suited her, and soon after he moved in. With great dispatch the Black Hole was transformed by her new lover into a den straight out of a Sculley & Sculley mail-order catalogue; not a trace of David remained.

But you know how it is once you start missing someone you haven't seen in a long time. Sara started wondering what David was up to and tried to reach him, but found he had moved without a forwarding address. Passing through the hall of her apartment, she paused as she passed the reflection of a girl in the oval mirror. Who could it be? – so goes magic.

HAZEL KELLY
IN FULL PURSUIT

A man passing stopped me, walking on a crowded
city street in Chicago.
    "Miss – are you Hazel Kelly?"
    "No, I'm not."
    I hastened on.
    Later I realized I should have said—
    "Yes, yes I am."
    and slipped into another life.

THE WOODBOX

It's winter and I'm in Paris on a business trip with Bill, my husband of thirty years. He is sprawled out beside me, soundly sleeping while I lie in the Ritz Hotel at dawn unable to sleep. Actually, dawn hasn't come yet, and the velvet portiers pulled across the French windows looking onto the Cambon side of the Ritz make the room so dark I can't see a thing, but I know dawn is about to break, a sparrow in the garden below started a waking call, then another, and now other sparrows are back and forth to each other. I know the map of every island and valley this bed is capable of becoming and just when I think I've discovered a new spot the pillow sinks back to a place I've already been. It's when the sparrows started up my mind drifted to someone I hadn't thought of in forty years – Jerry. His stationery was a linen weave – gray, with a faint plaid pattern – and printed in a subtle red on top and flap of the envelope was

Gerald M.T. Smith, 94 Palmer Square, Princeton, NJ, as trembling I would open his letters. My boarding school chums at Miss Wheelock thought it the most elegant stationery they'd ever seen – of course they'd seen the picture I had on top of the bureau in the room I shared with snooty Miriam Darlington. Even she was impressed. Many had beaux, but none as good looking plus he was "an older man" – nineteen – but this letter was in pencil – "Darling, I'm so happy that you got the weekend off as reward for keeping your room neat and tidy, but I knew you'd get it all along anyway, so all I am now is just happier. I will now come up Friday late and register at The Biltmore, GMT Smith. We can be there Saturday morning. Then I can get a car and we can go driving in the afternoon – darling, I just had an amazing idea. Why not get out of Providence right away and go down to Jamestown for the day! Nobody's at the house – the catch is that the house is closed for winter and unless we break in (I don't know how) we will arouse suspicion and it'll be risky. I'm trying to think how this can be done as it's a terrific idea – just think honey we can buy some sandwiches for lunch and I'll bring my portable radio and we can build a fire and be all, all alone

cozy and warm – oh honey, how wonderful. If I
only had the keys or a key to a door – how stupid
of me never to think of this before. Let's see (the
important thing is not to be seen or recognized). If
we break in, or even leave a car out in front, the
police would get suspicious and that would be
worse; and if I wire or write Joan for keys, God
knows, but any story might get out or at least people might be on the lookout, seeing how it's an
island – *Later. 11 o'clock Tuesday night.* Darling, I
think I have everything all worked out. I have wired
mother and already received an answer as to Joan's
address in Jamestown; and I will now write the letter to the effect that I am coming up to get some
important papers etc. out of The Woodbox. I will
then tell her to leave the keys with Pitcher's Drug
Store for me (as I'll say I don't know when exactly
I'll arrive), and when we get to Jamestown I will
leave you for a second at the house (up on the
porch) and run down, pick up the keys as if I were
alone, and no one will know the difference. If any-
body comes we'll be inside and I'll just shoo them
away saying that I've important work to attend to.
At this point I can't find any flaws in this plan and
nobody will even be suspicious of anything going

on. After your Aunt Allie calls for you at school we can tell her that we're going to visit those friends of mine I stayed with before in Newport and that will be excuse enough for her – so I think everything is wonderful now. Pookie, it's going to be such fun as there'll be no light, water or anything (and we'll have to find a potty in the attic for wee-wee!).

"Pookie angel I love you sometimes even more than those five letters you get a day but I must say good night as I've got to write Joan now and mail everything.

Aruf

Jerry

P.S. Joan is fat little maid."

Jerry starting the car. Aunt Allie waving us off as we began talking in whispers. Not that we were scared. Not for one minute. I'd never been so happy and excited in my life. I didn't have to be back at school until Sunday morning at ten and until then I'd be with Jerry as if we were married, living in a house of our own. I was so happy I even allowed myself to pretend I was scared – a little – that something would happen to stop us having this day. No one can do that unless they are terribly terribly sure that nothing can. I just knew it couldn't, because if it did – I'd just die! I kept trying to get him to drive faster and kept looking back once in a while to reassure him that no one was following. It was winter, as it is now here in Paris, and cold. I was wearing a lavender sweater buttoned down the front and a skirt I'd had especially dyed to match. The sweater had my initials in white on the left side and it was Jerry's favorite because he liked the color on me. I wore it over a crinkly white coat which looked vaguely like lambswool only it wasn't, but it certainly did look awful with the plaid beret Jerry had given me for Christmas. He had one exactly like it and I was crazy about that cap and he'd be wearing his, so I was thrilled to wear mine. It looked marvelous on him, mine did too, only sometimes, well, it just didn't go with the lavender and white rest of me. I felt funny in those days in clothes. They never quite rested easily on my skin the way they do now. It was a couple of hours drive from Providence until we got to the ferry that would take us to Jamestown. I'd never seen the island at that time of year and it was almost deserted. On the ferry there was only one other couple and a woman with a dog on a leash.

They got out of their cars and leaned on the railing staring over the water. The dog too — we stayed in the car but it wouldn't have made any difference if we hadn't. No one said a word or even looked at anyone else. Not even when we landed as we huddled together and tried not to giggle. While waiting on the porch for Jerry to get the key from Pitcher's Drug Store I tried to see through a slat in the shutters into the living room of the house his parents called The Woodbox. It looked different. I'd been there the summer before for a weekend to meet his mother and father. It was heaven, but now even more. Jamestown had nothing to do with the island as I'd remembered it in summer. The clapboard houses close by faded into the monotone of sea gray water and sky. Nothing existed now but The Woodbox and me outside looking through the shutters, into the living room, knowing Jerry would arrive any minute with the key. When we got inside the house the first thing Jerry did was take me in his arms. God, the way it was when he kissed me. That perilous sweetness — no me, only melting into Jerry. Then he started getting wood to make a fire. As he put the logs on, he stopped to look up at me with a look he sometimes had that kept reminding me of, something. Only I

still couldn't think what? I know, I said. A pie. A
pie? he said laughing, looking away. Yes – that's just
what it's like! Why a pie – I don't know? I said, it's
the only way I can describe it. I laughed and started
pulling the dust sheets off the sofa. Soon the room
looked as if we had been living in it forever. Jerry
had brought a hamper with a whole cold chicken in
it and peanut butter and jelly sandwiches. Lots of
other things too. Macaroons and hard-boiled eggs.
Milk and pickles. Even a red tablecloth with red and
white checked napkins that matched. We were so
happy we weren't hungry. We pushed the furniture
around so that the sofa was in front of the fire, lay
down together, and started kissing again. This time
into oblivion – where we remained the whole day,
stopping only to come up for air, or to put a log on
the fire. He'd look at me, watching the flames light
my face, touching my hair, and I reached out to
him, tracing the outline of his face to imprint it on
my heart forever. I'd want his lips again, then he'd
want more, and I would too – all that day, that's
how it was. And all that night the same, without
stopping. Then it got really dark, only I have no
idea when, or what time it was. The fire burned
down for the hundredth time, and it was colder, so

he went for more logs to keep the fire going. I couldn't bear him being not beside me. Hurry back darling hurry, I called after him. While he was gone it came over me how hungry I was. How hungry he must be too. I opened the hamper and spread the cloth on the floor in front of the fireplace and when he came back every bit of food was spread out. Nothing ever tasted so good. We'd almost finished when he remembered he'd brought a radio – and into the room that lovely melody – "You-are-the-promised-kiss-of-springtime-that-makes-the-lone-ly-winter-seem-long—" filled the room as we danced – funny, it's the only song I remember when after, we sat gazing into the fire, not talking except sometimes drifting into the future, how it would be when we were married, every day together, forever and ever. Towards dawn we must have slept a little; I remember waking without knowing I'd been asleep. All around The Woodbox birds were singing, although it was still dark outside – singing, just as they are now. They woke Jerry and I remember him turning over – and the way his hand felt as my breast turned to meet it. How they sang those birds, as light started to filter through the shutters into the room just as they are now through the portiers. How they sang.

All around The Woodbox – all around us, through dawn without stopping. The sound of that singing with Jerry's arms around me – oh God – I'd never forget it. Yet I did.

LURES

Doubtless if there is a place of peace Alice has found it. Health, reasonable wealth, contentment her son has found his calling, a successful writing career, house with a garden, a beloved dog, supportive friends, and a lover who shared delight in taking her swing dancing. She even considered herself prettier now that she was at peace instead of young and wild with a yearning that did not seem to end. She had come to suspect there is no *it*, there's just the longing For *it*.

Until one spring morning, scanning the *New York Review of Books* "Personal Services" she came upon this:

> Woman seeking mother: Motherless Daughter orphaned at 10, looking to forge a mother-daughter understanding, greater NYC. Married, caring, creative, educated writer, avid reader, 39, loves conversation, dogs, dance, gardening. Martha's Vineyard. Seekingmother@aol.com

It was a message she had been waiting for.

Fatherless, abandoned by her mother when she was ten, Alice had been raised in foster homes. Later she had experienced with her husband (until his death) and son a family life, sensing what it would have been to have the love of supportive family. After her son was born she miscarried and in the depression that followed became convinced the loss was the daughter she had longed for. He cautioned it would be difficult to have another child. Instead of deterring her, it strengthened her resolve to give birth to a daughter. It would put right, in her fantasy, the relationship with the mother she had lost.

To ease her depression she "adopted" through a charitable organization an infant girl in Vietnam stipulating she be born the same month of the child she had miscarried. A photograph of the baby was sent and through the organization she started correspondence with the child's family. But it was unsatisfactory. She felt no connection to her "adopted" daughter. She stopped writing, but kept sending checks. The void remained.

Then Alice heard about a fertility drug, Pergonol, banned in the United States by the FDA but available in Italy, where anyone could walk in a pharmacy and buy without a prescription. She was on a plane the next day to Rome and hours later on a return flight to New York, the illegal drug strapped with adhesive tape around her waist, concealed by a flowing muumuu. Nothing could have deterred her quest and with nerveless poise she serenely slipped through Customs without incident. It was too late.

But was it?

She the "motherless daughter" orphaned at ten (Alice's age when abandoned by her own mother).

She the "writer, avid reader, 39" (Alice's age the year *her* mother died).

She the daughter "looking to forge a mother-daughter understanding." *Now*, full circle, *She* has become the mother that "woman seeking mother" is waiting for.

Alice walked through the house she had created, filled with books, pictures, objects and colors she loved – home. She hesitated—

Rest easy, rest easy. Don't! Danger!

She went into the garden and sat beside a little pond stocked with goldfish. It calmed as she dipped her hand out to the fish leisurely drifting in the shadowy depths. Suddenly the sun hit the crystal ring she always wore, and a fish leapt towards the chimera of light.

It was the *signal* she had been waiting for.

AN EGG

I was an egg. The shell broke and out came the yolk. It was Susanna, but she was known as Susie until she died. At ten. Later I had another daughter and I named her Susan. It was confusing – a mistake. But as time passed she came to resemble Susanna. I knew I could have no more children. But as Susan grew more and more like Susanna I came to believe that Susanna hadn't died. So maybe it wasn't a mistake after all?

BURNE-JONES
AND MICKEY MOUSE

Jill is an artist who drives herself from dawn to dusk. Her closest friends are Mimi and Rachel, and she has a lover who more fully lives far enough away so as not to intrude on her work. He comes and goes, and only lately has started to get on her nerves.

When Jill isn't overworking she spends time on email or the phone with Rachel, who lives in Los Angeles, or with Mimi who lives close by in New York, or with her lover who lives in Kansas City. He has met both Mimi and Rachel, but Rachel and Mimi have not met. Each are diametrically opposite in character and temperament so Jill depends on both to confer about her lover; they react with disparate points of view so it gives her a lot to ruminate on as she spins their remarks to suit herself.

Rachel, an actress resembling a woman rendered by the English painter Burne-Jones (a great beauty capable of a haunting plainness). Her career flounders as she turns down parts that bring other actresses Academy Awards. Although they are the same age Jill is motherly towards her, but occasionally finds the roles reversed – she the child, Rachel the mother. This is puzzling to Jill as she has cut off contact with her mother, whom she has not seen or heard from in years. Mimi, with a new job at a fashion magazine, appears somewhat manufactured, having transformed herself from a feisty Mickey Mouse cartoon into an image of take-charge beauty the magazine promotes.

"It's odd," Jill's lover said the last time he'd seen her, "—you pick friends so different from each other."

"What do you mean by that?" she'd replied defensively.

"I don't know – Rachel: fragile, wicky-wacky – I happened to be in L.A. that time she cut her wrists; the other one, Mimi – tough as nails – they'd hate each other on sight."

Jill is infuriated with her lover for taking it upon himself to judge her friends; they end up fighting. "You've got it all wrong. Mimi is the fragile one – think how sensitive she has to be to juggle beauty and business working for a fashion magazine, and Rachel – she's the tough one; think of the breakdowns she's bounced back from."

Since they met, Jill has studied Mimi, imitating the tawny coloring of her hair styled in a fuzz around the energy of a fierce little face. Mimi advises her about trends in cosmetics, clothes and colors which best suit the porcelain skin they share. Her worldly pursuits intrigue Jill. She tacks a picture of herself next to one of Mimi on the door of the refrigerator, "Hey twin – now I've found you I'll never let you go."

"I'm going to paint you," Jill tells Mimi and she works obsessively on the portrait. "You know how fast I work – no posing – it's already in my head."

But at the end of a fevered day, sitting back to study results, centered on the canvas, a blurred face resembling Rachel appears. How can that be? There is nothing in character or appearance about the take-charge Mimi that relates to the ethereal Rachel. Fond as she is of Rachel, her opinions often annoy Jill and to avoid arguments she sometimes stops listening.

Jill attacks the canvas again, determined that it become a portrait of Mimi. But when finished, this time, it more than likely resembles someone else – her mother. Taking the canvas off the easel she puts it facing against the wall before taking her brushes to clean in the sink.

Mimi tells her she can't wait to see her portrait, but Jill says she's so busy she hasn't had time to begin. A few weeks later she takes another look at the painting and is about to email Rachel in Los Angeles to be on the lookout for a surprise on its way, but instead she protects the portrait in bubble wrap and sends it on to her mother.

GREEN DREAM

This is it: My lover Roberto has died, or so I am led to believe. Coolly observing my grief, Doreen, his former lover (who I am dangerously jealous of), takes pity and reveals that she is the only one who knows his death has been fabricated to punish me for past indiscretions (what?). Distraught, I plead to know his whereabouts. Moved by my hysteria, she intimates this is unknown to anyone but herself. On my knees I beg for information. "Shut up," she says, slapping duct tape over my mouth. "You'll *never* find him." Weird noises emanate from me as I wake sobbing to find Roberto rocking me in his arms. "Hush, my treasure, hush, it was only a dream." We make passionate love and I am assuaged, but not for long.

Weeks pass as the dream pops up, repeating itself in alarming sequence. But lately as I wake Roberto is not holding me in his arms. He is shaking my shoulder, mumbling, "For Christ's sake, go back to sleep."

What is the significance of this dream? Is it a messenger of signs and portents? Something to do with the dreaded Doreen's infatuation for Roberto? My voices compel me, find out. Not an easy task. She never took to me from the beginning. Surprised at how calculating I become determined to get a wee toehold into her world. It's not in my nature to be jealous. How could it be, growing up with Dad telling me I was a beauty, and even if Mom, in her downswings, told me it was a damn lie, I knew it was only so I wouldn't get out of hand, go off the deep end the way she often did. I could always count on her to bounce up again, concurring with Dad that I was the prettiest, smartest girl in town. Later, when I became a model, I held my head high with the best – and if ever I doubted, I'd hear the echo of Dad's voice, "Remember, you're as good as the best thing you've ever done."

Although Doreen is quite a bit older than Roberto, when we first met I thought they were a couple to be admired. I was stunned when Roberto started taking an interest in me. "What about Doreen?" He was nonplussed: "What *about* her?" I was so in love it didn't give pause, but this recurrent dream which has me in thrall is the red flag as to how mistaken I was not to have taken heed, probed deeper instead of jumping up and down clapping my hands, singing out, Yes! Yes! Yes! instead of stomping my foot and saying No! No! No!

My campaign accelerates as I start inviting Doreen out for lunch, and finally, instead of reciprocating by inviting me to fancy restaurants, she invites me to her townhouse. Goggle-eyed I gaze around her garnet-red dining room as we dine on smoked trout, petit pois, and chardonnay, looking out into a garden – in summer, lacy-green, in winter, bushes heavy with snow appear as if sculpted into hostile snowmen. We talk of this and that and these lunches usually dawdle on into the dinner hour. I realize that Doreen is much more brilliant and intelligent than I had given her credit for. We do look more than somewhat alike, although I am fair and she is dark, close enough to be mistaken for sisters, even twins perhaps except for her overweight problem. She is one of those who blow up and down so you never know what you're up against. Fat or thin Doreen is chock-a-full with secrets about Roberto, which I keep trying to wheedle out of her. Secrets I will never be part of because they are knotted together in a tight fist – I'd be KO'd in the first round. This bond far more intense than either one of them let on, and might last far longer than any future history Roberto and I can look forward to. Despite my jealousy, as I get closer to Doreen I become quite fond of her, and question if this recurrent dream is swinging me onto a wrong track? Was I being unfair? But wait. The very next day Roberto said, "Doreen taught me everything I know about grace and beauty." I wanted to slap him and scream – that's *my* department. Prudently I kept silent, but it hit hard and from then on green poison oozed into the very air I breathed.

Right now Doreen's not only overweight – in the circles we move in she's considered borderline obese and somewhat dowdy. Except her house is elegant, I grant. Endlessly weighing pros and cons, I face defeat. She *is* smarter than I am. Devious and worldly in a way I can never be because, as I already told you, it's not in my nature to have vile traits – meanness and jealousy, and soon my obsession takes chunks out of my heart as I observe how cleverly she draws people to her. No surprise she has so many more friends than I do. Don't think I'm imagining it when I sense people perceive me to be an ice princess, when in actuality I'm a hot tamale. It's just difficult – nay, impossible – for me to crack out of my shell except in moments of making love with Roberto, my beloved Roberto, my caro mio, or shouldn't I say *our* caro mio (Doreen's and mine) for surely as day is night he is fast slipping away from me. And why not? Doreen has none ·of my waspy hang-ups – from the moment I met her with Roberto she was on to me, knew that he would be attracted by my neediness and might enjoy a romp around in the playpen with me to work out his own hang-ups – yes – two needys locked in the playpen would eventually bond, but all too soon he would miss Doreen's strong fist, for they are a coin – he, I was fast learning, the weaker side.

Frenzied with jealousy, the more inventive my courtship becomes: creatively consulting her about Roberto as he distances himself more frequently and the dream – like a serial killer – relentlessly comes and goes, goes and comes.

Still, I was flattered when she went on a diet, curious to how we models kept so skinny; it was me she consulted. I watched mesmerized as the lard sloughed off her fat body. How could it disappear so quickly? But disappear it did. In no time at all, side by side, standing like schoolgirls, stark naked, giggling at ourselves in front of the tall mirror in her dressing room, we stood eerily, exactly, at six feet. Later, taking turns up and down on the scale, our weights an equal 115 pounds. I had to take deep breaths in and out, out and in, to calm myself, so excited when asked my opinion about clothes. This was the opportunity I had been waiting for: Eagerly I advised her to wear green, but it has to be the right green. Of course, whatever green she chose it would never be the right green because green just isn't her color. It's mine. Her name, Doreen, should also belong to me, because it rhymes with green, but no matter – the more involved we became – jealousy accelerates. What good Dad's advice now? Doreen has far outdistanced me in anything I could ever achieve – Roberto.

Consumed by murderous thoughts I purge soaking in a scalding hot bath, encouraged to see veins on my hands, arms and legs turning green (bet she can't do that). My hazel eyes litmus paper taking on a greener hue. To accentuate the effect I emerge from the bath to rub myself with creamy green body lotion. Imitating Doreen, I start amassing an overextended green wardrobe – sweaters, blouses, gloves, hose – to enhance the effect, along with an extensive collection of boots and shoes. Each detail given careful consideration – yes, green angora booties to keep my tootsies warm at night, such a comfort when Roberto is away on one of his covert missions. My credit card spirals out of control with Doreen going into full throttle, outdoing my passion in competing for emerald jewels to compliment the look. Her choices however inevitably overburdened with the wrong green – jade – just don't cut it. I applaud her efforts as each addition diminishes the desired effect, although her sycophant friends keep egging her on, telling her how great she looks.

Now I know it is true – what Mom, sage Mom, kept drilling into me, during those years I kept struggling to create myself. The moon *is* made of green cheese, no matter how Dad said to stop putting crazy notions in my head. Free at last when night falls to gaze up, as the copycat stars follow suit and green twinkles fall around and about like confetti on New Year's Eve, giving brief respite from the dream that still stalks. Other twinkles too along the way – at Bloomingdales I pounce upon a green nail polish, trembling as I apply the lacquer to my nails,

as green butterflies drift in and out of my mind, deli-
ciously distracting as their delicate wings bump into
each other, urging me to heed their tender murmur-
ings and not go off on a wild goose chase which I
tend to do more and more lately, whispering they
dart in and out, out and in counseling me on ways
to choke Doreen – or better still, set her on fire.

Hard to believe, but it's not Doreen who goes up
in flames. It's my life, my love, my beloved, in a car
accident. Only ashes left. It is Doreen, who remains
sexy and sinewy – devoted Doreen, friend and constant companion together we mourn until after the
funeral, shock! She informs she is moving *somewhere* – permanently. A joke, surely? She whisks me
off to JFK to wish her bon voyage, where, dazed, I
stand watching her board a plane, clutching a green
alligator tote bag in one paw without even a look
back to wave Bye Bye with the other.

Hotfooting it back to the city, I hire a limo to
gad about hither and yon in New Jersey, contacting
my medical advisors, gathering prescriptions for
sleeping pills. No matter shape or size, green they
must be. Home in bed I drop into the well of
dreamless sleep – the serial killer at bay. But wake
sobbing.

I have a compulsion to stuff these pages in one of the empty green bottles of chardonnay that somehow have taken possession of my kitchen, accumulating like relics I can't bear to throw away. Yes! Seal the bottle up – into the ocean. I'm on my way there right now to do just that. Myself along with it – why not? We can bob along together in the sea – the bitter green sea that makes me suspect I am homeless and have no roof but dreams – side by side, bobbing along together until we turn up on some beach somewhere. And this time I *am* going to kill her.

LATER, MARY?

At a black-tie dinner party of strangers someone called Jason sits on my right with Mary, his wife, across from me at the table. Soon I will be married to a man none of us knows exists. Later Mary will marry this man and be with him until he dies. Jason will be forgotten.

CARTOON CHARACTERS IN SEARCH OF A MODUS VIVENDI

Daddy Warbucks and Snow White are a couple who project energy, beauty and power. He, puffed up, affluent, exuding success. She, exquisite, dainty, hair styled into a prim chignon, but up-to-the-minute in the latest fashion, yet never snooty, always modest, reserved, sweet. Hand in hand the couple enter rooms and spirits lift! Much gossiped about – "He's a different person when he's with Snow White than he is when he's with The Little King." But how exactly? Friends find it hard to define. It's mean to refer to the other in that way – squat, square, long robe, pageboy bob cartoon sporting a tiny crown, but so accurate it's irresistible. Well, the comparison wasn't Snow White's idea. It's not in her nature to be mean. Or is it? Still, although she kept quiet about it, she couldn't help puzzle as did their friends – what was going on? What glue held together this arrangement Daddy Warbucks had so deftly orchestrated?

And why, as the months passed, did Snow White and The Little King put up with it? This was an enigma? But then so was Daddy Warbucks. Where exactly had he sprouted from? But sprout he had. From nowhere forming a computer business, Pie In The Sky Ltd., Inc., millions rolling in as he aggressively leapt into the social scene, managing everything with the same determination as he did his leisure time.

Recently Daddy Warbucks had taken The Little King on a vacation to Yama Yama Land. Now it was time to reward Snow White, gallantly encouraging her to choose where? Puerto Vallarta. And here we come upon them, their vacation over, seated in the back of a car as the driver makes his way toward the airport on their way back to New York.

Daddy Warbucks studies Snow White gazing out the window as they drive along the highway. How unpredictable she is, he muses – that morning, bewitching as a Geisha girl, relating an incident of the night before. She may have charmed in the telling, but it had been much more than an incident. Preparing for bed, sitting barefoot at the dressing table – a bug emerged from under the chair, crawled over her bare toes, meandering over the white tile floor, disappearing under the door of the bathroom. Screaming, she jumped onto the bed, reaching for the phone to call Daddy Warbucks in his room down the hall. They had been out in the cantinas, enjoying margaritas, tripping the light fantastic until God knows when. Odd, his line was busy? She kept staring at the door where the bug had vanished. Temped to go down the corridor, knock on his door, she hesitated, fearful the bug might emerge while she was gone – be waiting upon her return. Even with Daddy Warbucks by her side she couldn't face another encounter. She lay in bed, lights on until dawn, distracting herself by irreverently examining her relationship with Daddy Warbucks and The Little King. Way, way back she journeyed, back when, dazzled by Daddy Warbucks' charisma, she let herself slip into this unfortunate liaison. What did it matter that he had informed her The Little King had been put on notice – "If you *ever* try to break up my relationship with Snow White I'll leave you." She could hear his sonorous voice saying this and remembered how foolishly happy it made her. But could not those words have been juxtaposed to accommodate The Little

King, "If Snow White ever tries to break up *our* relationship I'll leave her." How like Daddy Warbucks to invent this Trio to puff up his macho image. The Little King: fat, eminently suitable for fucking. Snow White: slim, eminently suitable for showing off. It made her raging-boiling-pissed-off-mad. She tried calming herself by recalling cherished ceremonies they'd shared: toasting each other with rosé wine he enjoyed, cow eyes gazing into hers, clicking glasses whispering, "L'amour, toujours l'amour." Had this ceremony been shared with The Little King? Even if it hadn't – how trite, how meaningless, how hollow, as she repeated it in the lonely room.

❅

Next morning on the terrace overlooking the sea, breakfasting on coffee and huevos rancheros, Snow White strained to amuse him recounting her adventure.

"But why didn't you call me? We could have exchanged rooms."

"But there might have been a bug in your room too," she flirted. "Anyway I did, but your line kept busy."

"Well, the concierge, certainly his line wouldn't be busy."

"That never occurred to me – you know what good manners I have," she said archly. "Perhaps I didn't want to embarrass him, suggesting such a thing could happen in a five-star hotel."

"The margaritas, perhaps?" he said, winking.

"Not necessarily."

❅

On the way to the airport, lulled by the drone of the car, Daddy Warbucks and Snow White dozed in the backseat. Suddenly the car jolted as she was thrown upright, stunned to see The Little King sitting in the seat beside the driver.

"Yikes! Daddy Warbucks – look," Snow White shook his arm, "look there – look, sitting in front."

"What?" he said, leaning forward. "I don't see anything."

He was right. There was nobody. A passing car for a blink tricked the empty headrest and seat into the illusion that a fat person sat in front of them.

"Relax, baby, too much sun – last night's bugs, manana, whatever. Oh hell, I'm tired too, but what a time we had – terrif, wasn't it!" he took her hand and squeezed it. "I loves ya – ya knows I do."

But she isn't listening and pulls her hand away.

THE GOLD DUST TWINS

Two women sit on a banquette in a Turkish corner at the Café Carlyle on a spring afternoon. One is Daisy Balfour, still dazzling, and the other Sally Wentworth, hair wispy from too much bleaching, but bravely pressing on. For one reason or another, Sally has always been jealous of Daisy. Not only because she became a movie star and married a millionaire, but mainly because of Terry Dunne's continuing preoccupation with Daisy, her closest friend since childhood.

In spite of this, and although they had recently avoided one another for years, when they ran into each other by chance on Madison Avenue there were cries and hugs, which is how they find themselves at the Carlyle talking about old times and getting poodled.

"What have you been up to, Sally?" Daisy sinks back into the banquette as Sally fiddles with her hair.

"Oh, since my husband died..." she trailed off, "funny he died the same year yours – I thought of calling but—"

"Wish I'd known, I'd have called *you*."

"Actually – it was a relief – the suffering."

"Oh darling." Daisy reaches out for Sally's hand, but Sally looks away and the gesture becomes a signal to the waiter for another chardonnay.

"Are you still on Sutton Place?"

"Oh Sally – has it been that long since we've seen each other? – no, a building went up blocking my view. I moved to Fifth with a view of the park – *that'll* be there a while—"

"I moved too – couldn't bear to live in the house in Nyack after my husband died. I'm cozily ensconced in Soho. What about you, Daisy? Do you ever see any of the old Hollywood crowd? Oh, my – the fun we had!"

"Not really – you know how it is – 'other voices, other rooms.'"

"And Terry?"

"Terry?"

"Yes – Terry Dunne."

"Jesus, Sally – why bring him up!"

"Well, it split our friendship—"

"Sally – look at me – you and I know Terry was certifiable – nutty as a fruitcake – dangerous."

"How can you say that? Eccentric – but – dangerous?"

"If you'd ever been strapped with him on a motor-cycle going a hundred miles an hour—"

"There were no motorcycles around when I dated him." Sally sounds surprised.

"Let's not go there, Sally—"

Sally takes another sip of chardonnay and wishes to God she hadn't skipped lunch. "No – let's. I want to, I really do."

"Please—" Daisy rolls her eyes – "when I have insomnia I count my lovers instead of sheep and he's the one I skip over."

"You're being unfair, Daisy."

"Those brawls, the publicity – that time he walked into St. Patrick's naked – how about that?"

"He never was a drunk when he was with me," Sally says smugly.

"And certainly not with me—"

"So don't exaggerate—"

"Oh come on, it's what ruined his acting career."

Sally grabs Daisy's hand. "But I knew I could save him." All she gets from Daisy is a wave of her hand

and a raised eyebrow. "Stop looking at me like that, Daisy."

"I'm not looking at you 'like that,' Sally, but if I am it's because you and I know, he was in love with me first, and if being in love with Daisy Balfour couldn't save him – nothing could."

"He *was* nuts about you, but, but—" Sally woozily swirls into Daisy's glamour.

"I suppose so," Daisy shrugs.

"I don't suppose – I know."

"But he hadn't gotten to know me yet and—"

"We were having fun," Daisy interrupted. "No more than that. But the rough stuff – that's what really put me off."

"Rough stuff – what do you mean rough stuff?"

"Come on, you know what I mean."

"Never! Always tender and sweet – might we say it may have been you, Daisy – drove him—"

"Sally – you can't mean that."

"I do, I do – it's why I never wanted to see you again – yes, after you dumped him – I knew when he started seeing me it was because you were my best friend and it kept him close to you – his not being able to forget you made it like he was cheating on me – see what I mean?"

"Who's your therapist, Sally?"

"I don't have one – I have a guru."

"Well you need to seriously confer with him."

"It's not a him – it's a her."

"Whatever."

"It took a lot of – you know – wheedling – to get Terry to even see her—"

"And?"

"It set him off again."

"I never could get it? Why you were so intense about him – well he was good looking, until booze and: poof, gone with the wind."

Sally closes her eyes and leans back against the banquette, murmuring, "eyes like steel found me – made me sense that I could be the stream to feed the roots – for my love seemed like a tree – needing a strange alchemy – from my eyes green moss – absorbing his eyes – that shut me out."

"What the hell is that?"

"It's a poem I wrote—" tears come and she takes a tissue from her purse. "He cherished them – yes he did."

"Sounds like the drivel he used to write to me when they put him in the funny farm in Palm Springs."

"Do you still have them?"

"Silly Sally, of course not – and stop blubbering." Daisy hands her a handkerchief from her purse.

"Mine are in a box inlaid with mother of pearl – even the ones written on paper napkins," she said proudly.

"How touching," Daisy said.

"You're horrid and mean, Daisy—"

"Lighten up – just kidding."

Sally started to get up.

"Come on – one more for the road – you always did take things too seriously."

"I really *do* have to go, Daisy. I'm late. Actually, I'm meeting Terry."

"Why you little faker," Daisy laughed, "I thought he was still in prison."

"Well he's *not* – he's out on parole. I didn't get into that – testing what you might say. I always was the better actor – even if my career never took off the way yours did."

"But I had the tits, darling," Daisy laughed. "So you did save him after all – goody for you."

"I got him right smack into AA – the day he got out of prison and it's working. Yes, definitely."

"His health?"

"The coughing's better, but I still can't get him off two packs a day. Nightmares – now and then … tossing, mumbling."

"Mumbling what?"

"Just gibberish."

"Not – 'Daisy, Daisy, give me your answer do?'" she sings.

"Oh I have missed you," Sally gave Daisy a mock punch on her shoulder – "I really have – you always could make me laugh. Remember how everybody called us the Gold Dust Twins? And here we are, still little girls, but all grown up."

"True, true," Daisy said, signaling for the check.

When they got out onto the street it was already dark.

"Can I drop you somewhere?" Sally said.

"No thanks, darling, I live right around the corner."

"I love you, Daisy." Sally gave her a hug.

"I love you too, Sally."

"We'll never lose each other again – in constant communication from now on?"

"Of course, Sally, of course!"

"Of course."

Sally got into a taxi and rolled down the window, waving to Daisy as she walked towards Fifth Avenue, but Daisy didn't look back and they never saw each other again.

MY DARLING
FROM THE LIONS

One summer morning, as the sun ascended over the city, Daisy Balfour stepped from a scented bath, put on a terry robe, and stood looking out the window at the building across the street which had been mushrooming up since early spring. Its progress had been observed apprehensively, for soon it would shoot up, partially obscuring her view of the East River. *Oh me oh my, where will I live when the world goes dark?* she shrugged, sighed. Venturing forth onto the terrace as every morning, to a secret island, a chaise with down cushions covered in a linen poppy print, strategically placed under a flowering tree where no one from river or street could find her. Flickering dappled light shadowed across the beauty of her body as she threw aside the robe and stretched out on the chaise. But soon, from construction on the building, the relentless riveting began.

"Stop – make them stop!" she shouted to Enid, her maid, who glided towards her bearing a tray of the usual breakfast – fruit salad and black coffee. As if Enid waved a wand – abruptly the riveting stopped. She set the tray on a table beside the chaise, nodded and retreated back into the penthouse. Everything settled into silence until cutting through the heat Daisy heard whistles – her name shouted – there was no mistaking it. Overnight the vantage points had shifted. Workers on the building across the street could now look down onto where she lay stretched out on her terrace – *Run rabbit run,* round and around her mind raced in a maze but each path led to where she lay trapped. If they hadn't recognized her, an unknown woman sunning on a city terrace would have jumped into a robe and scurried quickly on into the house. What of it? Quickly forgotten. But this was different. She was a known person and these strangers calling, whistling at her as she lay naked before them, invaded, knew her intimately. It would stay with her and them, forever. *Rescue my soul from their destruction, my darling from the lions* – she lay paralyzed as the chorus continued – instinctively, not knowing why, she sat up, reached up to touch the sun filtering through the leaves. *I'll make my body a sieve, a sieve so that the hurt will pass as water through me* – moving slowly she tossed the robe aside and sauntered on across the terrace. Opening the door to her bedroom, pausing to look back to where the men stood hooting at her, calling her name, staring past them as though they did not exist. She turned to face them for a few moments. Suddenly it was quiet – as if it had been a bad dream she'd had dozing off in the morning sun. Pausing, she waited – and went on into the bedroom.

The room was cool and dark. She lay face up on the bed. The cat came and settled himself on her chest … her breath settling into the rhythm of his breathing. After a while she gently moved the cat onto a pillow and went into her dressing room, standing, critically examining the smooth skin on a body she'd worked hard to maintain. She sat at her dressing table and started getting ready for the day ahead – a lunch where she was to be guest speaker – *No one who knows me will know no one who knows me will know*, she kept repeating as she put on her makeup. The cat wandered in and sat looking at her.

THE THINGS
WE FEAR MOST

On a day in summer, walking on the street I felt faint, and, passing a movie theatre, I went in to cool off. Someone in the movie said, "The things we fear most have already happened to us." I went out feeling happy, but when I got home something terrible had happened.

Acknowledgements

Deepest thanks to Barry Callaghan for initiating
the *Carter V. Cooper Anthology Series*, which presents
those Canadian writers – emerging and/or at any
point in their career – shortlisted from Exile's
new annual short fiction competition.

My thanks to Michael Callaghan for his
care given to the design of this book.

My thanks to my agent Jeanne Carter.

I want to acknowledge the various kinds of help
I received from Anderson Cooper, Katie Arnold-Ratliff,
Ben Brantley, Jane Gunther, Nancy Biddle, Matthew Smyth,
Marti Stevens, Christopher Madkour, Diane Meredith Voltz,
Nydia Caro, G.G. Marley, Gladys Szápáry, Janet Ruttenberg,
Wendy Goodman, Aurélia Thiérrée, César Recio,
Caroline Weber, Leonor Ramirez, Paul Szápáry, Jeannette Watson,
Anne Longley, Andrew Slaby, Joyce Carol Oates,
Luisa Valenzuela, and Laurence Tancredi.

Special thanks to lifelong friend Ellen M. Violett.

Finally, my most heartfelt thanks go to
Amy Hempel, whose advice, editorial and otherwise,
is an integral part of this book.

Gloria Vanderbilt